P9-DBW-898

A NOTE ABOUT THE STORY

C. W. Hunter first came across this wonderfully colorful piece of Americana in the writings of Mr. R. M. Ward of Wautauga County, North Carolina. Ward had heard the tale from his grandfather Council Harmon in the late 1800s, when Harmon was in his late eighties. And Harmon had heard the tale from *his* grandfather, who said he'd learned it from the early settlers of the United States.

But this modest tale may have roots that are even more venerable than that! Dr. Charles Zug of the University of North Carolina at Chapel Hill pointed out to us several similarities between *The Green Gourd* and a Native American tale called "The Offended Rolling Stone," which also features an inanimate object come to life to cause trouble.

No one knows how directly connected these two tales are. But one thing is certain: With *The Green Gourd* Whitebird is pleased to introduce C.W. Hunter and the artist Tony Griego, whose zany illustrations will "witch ye sure."

Tomie dePaola, Creative Director
WHITEBIRD BOOKS

THE GREEN GOURD

A North Carolina Folktale
retold by C. W. HUNTER
illustrated by TONY GRIEGO

A WHITEBIRD BOOK
G. P. Putnam's Sons
New York

To Marion Oettinger

—C.W.H.

To Colleen and Nancy

—T.G.

G. P. Putnam's Sons, a division of The Putnam & Grosset Book Group,
200 Madison Avenue, New York, NY 10016.
Published simultaneously in Canada
Printed in Hong Kong by South China Printing Co. (1988) Ltd.
Book design by Gunta Alexander
Library of Congress Cataloging-in-Publication Data
Hunter, C. W. The green gourd : a North Carolina folktale / retold by
C. W. Hunter ; illustrated by Tony Griego.   p.   cm.   "A Whitebird book."
Summary: An old woman in need of a water dipper defies the old caution
not to pick green gourds before they're ripe and soon regrets it.
[1. Folklore—North Carolina.] I. Griego, Tony, ill. II. Title.
PZ8.1.H94Gr 1991   90-25882 CIP AC   398.22'09756—dc20
ISBN 0-399-22278-2

1 3 5 7 9 10 8 6 4 2
First impression

Long time back, an old woman lived across a rushin'
stream and up a holler.

One day while she was scoopin' water with her gourd dipper, she dropped it into the stream. Before she could yell "Oh, law!" the current carried that dipper clean away.

Now, she needed a dipper awful bad. So directly she went
to the gourd vine by her house.

It was loaded with dipper gourds, all green and glossy, like ornaments strung on a Christmas tree.

But not a one was ripe.

Now, thereabouts the saying went, ''Never pull a green
gourd afore it's ripe, or it'll witch ye sure.'' But the old woman
paid that no mind a-tall. She needed a dipper awful bad.

So she yanked a big green gourd off the vine, took it home and set it on a chair near the fireplace to dry.

Then she commenced churnin' butter to slap on her supper biscuits.

All was quiet, except for the creak of the butter churn.

Then—

Rrrrrumble—the green gourd rolled off the chair and onto the hearth—*fump!* The old woman fetched it and put it right back on that chair. And—*rum-rum-rum*—the green gourd rolled right off again and bounced onto the floor—*fump!*

"If'n you won't set peaceful on a chair," the old woman told
the green gourd, "you can set yourself on the mantelpiece."
And she popped that green gourd up there.

But just as she settled herself again to churn—oh, law!—
that ol' green gourd commenced to rumblin' and roarin' up
and down the mantelpiece. It was havin' itself a good ol' time,
fumpin' everything in sight.

Then it sailed through the air, made straight for the old
woman and commenced to fumpin' her on the head—FUMP!
FUMP! FUMP!

My, did she jump! She flew out the door and began runnin'
and squallin' her head off, just fit to be tied, with the green
gourd right behind, tryin' its level best to fump her again.
     The old woman ran by a panther's house.

"What's the matter?" asked the panther.

"Oh, law!" she cried. "A witchy green gourd's on my heels, and it's goin' to fump me sure!"

"Run on in here," said the panther. "I'll take care of *it*."

She hopped into the house and hid herself good. The green gourd sailed on in after her.

When the panther leaped for it, the green gourd fumped him a time or two. Knocked him completely lopsided. Then it aimed itself straight for the old woman.

"Leave off!" shouted the old woman. But the green gourd just kept comin'. So she lit out o' there right smart. And that green gourd came on, whizzin' through the air and hummin' like swarmin' bees—*hummmmmmmmmmmmm.*

The old woman put up a little hum of her own—YEEEEEEEEEK—and kept runnin' till she like to drop.

She came to a fox's house, screechin' like a whole bait o' panthers was after *her.*

"What's the matter?" asked the fox.

"A fractious green gourd's fixin' to fump me good!"

"Run on in here," said the fox. "And I'll fump *it!*"

She ran inside, lickety-chop, and the green gourd shot in
right behind her.

The fox snapped at it, and it twirled around and knocked
him broadside. FUMP! Then it went for the old woman.

"Leave off!" she shouted. And she lit right out o' there. That green gourd lit out too.

Down the road it went, a-swishin' and a-swattin' and

a-swingin', tryin' its dangdest to fump the old woman.
And the old woman kept a-rumblin' and a-tumblin' and
a-bumblin', tryin' to stay loose of that thing.

She came to a boy's house.

The boy asked, "What's the matter here?"

"Plenty!" she cried. "A green gourd's comin' to fump me good!"

"Run on in here, ma'am," he said. "I'll give that green gourd what-for!"

Now, the boy was small, but he was spry. When the green gourd poked its neck through the door and came ribblin' across the floor, fixed on fumpin' the old woman,

the boy jumped out from behind the door, screechin', "Look out for me, green gourd!"

And he sat on it and squashed it flat.
They both cheered at that.

The the old woman took a broom, swept the pieces into the fireplace and burned 'em. And danged if that ol' green gourd didn't put on a fireworks display the likes of which were never seen thereabouts, neither afore nor after. CRACK! WHACK! WHANG! went the green gourd. Then, with a fearsome, witchy cackle, it disappeared in green smoke.

"Well, honey," the old woman said to the boy, "you fixed that green gourd, sure enough. Now let's find the other critters and celebrate."

So they all loped back to her place and feasted on biscuits with homemade butter. (They licked their fingers too.)

Then the old woman waited a good spell to make herself a new gourd dipper. 'Cause she knew for a fact—*Never pull a green gourd afore it's ripe, or it'll witch ye sure.*

925055

10.47

	DATE DUE		
3A	SEP 2 4 1993	3C	OCT 0 6 '94
3E	OCT 1 1 1993	1E	OCT 1 7 '94
3E	OCT 1 3 1993	OCT 2 6 '94	2D
1?	OCT 2 1 1993	3E	NOV 0 3 '94
3E	NOV 1 1993	3B	NOV 2 5 '94
3E	NOV 5 1993		
3E	NOV 2 4 1993		
3A	MAR 4 1994		
3e	MAR 1 0 1994		
2E B	MAY 2 4 1994		
2C	MAY 3 1 1994		
C	OCT 2 6 '94		